The Crystal Tower

by

George A. Hart

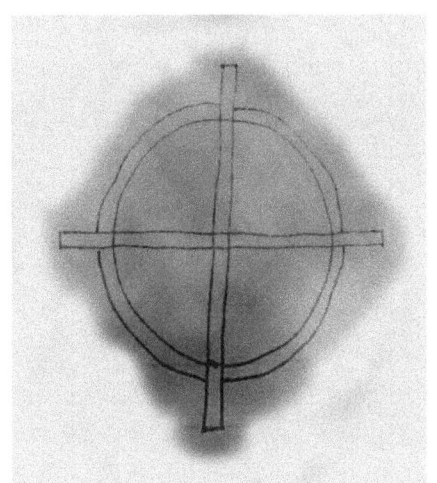

ISBN: 978-0-9840313-2-0

Introduction

This book was written when I was around 18 and 19 about in the years 1991 and 1992. I tried to fix my spelling errors, etc., the best I could without destroying the poetic quality of the book. This was probably my second or third short book written during my poem and song stage as I call it. I have always loved to make up my own words to describe things and that's something special I think a writer has a right to do. I believe it shows your uniqueness and maybe even talent. So, you'll find this book filled with my little creative aspects. This is a spiritual book which marks the beginning of my true spiritual path in my opinion. My other first books merely opened the door. This is the book where I actually stepped in, taking that leap of faith. So, I hope you enjoy this little journey through a teenagers mind. At this time (2006) I'm 33 and I look back at this and find it very interesting and strange. I first typed a copy up in my early 20's and mistakenly let a girl I knew take it to write it in calligraphy and to my surprise never seen it again. So, I'm finally getting around to retyping it and making it available to whoever wishes to read it. By the way this girl's name was Tina and she's one of the names I've blocked out at the end of the book in my dream. I think the others were Gayle and Stacie.

Who is man he who is flesh?
Why is he an where is his god?
What life does he hold?
A life without cause.
A god without truth.
A spirit without divinity.

Prologue

I stand to be the beginning of something old. By awakening my inner mind opening the path for man to learn. What his final achievement an life long destiny will ascertain. But you must learn on your own an be willing to work as one together. The column will be erected. It will stand to be the most important structure on this planet. Here an now known as earth. This book will be your guide to your spiritual plain. An the level of knowledge your will achieve. Experience the center, in your mind. An learn the answers to your own questions. Raising your intellectual capacity expanding your sense of divination. In turn strengthening your spiritual entity. For The Crystal Tower is rising.

(Original) Title Page: The Crystal Tower

This is the story of Atole.
Atole was a warrior.
A great warrior of the mind.
His power was beyond all reckoning.
He knew all things as they are in the state of being.
Time was only a myth as everything already was.
There he stalked the Lillan in its termination of Prod.
Prod sought vigilance from Lillan.
It's Lillan he betrayed all knowledge of the just.
He stood upon the platform Otar the varium for all thought.
An spoke the ancient words of Amen.
Amen wrote the first laws, The book of Amen.
This book was lost but the laws remembered.
Lillan discovered the book in a dark cave.
He deceived an twisted his words.
An befooled all that credits the League of Wisdom, LOW.
Defying every aspect that makes us proud.
Corrupting our very world The Kingdom of Low.
Making all prides an joys the founder of all un-wisdom.

Lillan I mock you who knows not his own end.
Hail your own death as you shall die from your own thought.
Woe an said he whoith is astray bare the mark of obedience.
An that you shall learn For I am Atole.
The master of all pure thought.
I shall come for you through this dream thought as life.
An find your increpit soul an squeeze the essence of time into reality.
Where you alone shall face its diseased infectious shades of morbid knowledge.
I shall cross into the wastelands in search of the now disbursed Prod.
You placed him in another dimension in four parts, Earth, Wind, Fire, Water.
For this great deed of terror deserves another I shall avenge my friend, mighty Prod.
There I'll place you in a hundred dimensions in a thousand parts.
You shall know my wrath for I am come, from out of the dark.

I am Atole I lived in the 4th corner of Low, Mentale.
Where I reigned over a people of the mind.
We were a peaceful nation living in total harmony.
There I saw the coming of Lillan.
Was there no solution yet to die?
We traveled to the center of Low.
To vast our knowledge upon the platform of Otar.
Where the four sections of Low meet.
Mentale, Awarenn, Concepta, Orderion.
This place is where the ancient counselers came.
To meet the four would stand upon the platform.
An complete their thought an end their disputes.
In another world their minds traveled to an beyond.
It became more a reality in time.
For then all at once Amen became part of our three minds.
He went in too far as he seen the soul of our god Wisdom.
His knowing cast our thoughts to nothing.
We are the creators, all things from the mind.
The knowledge separated into us three.
Along with Amen all of Concepta disappeared.
Causing chaos for our unit is broken.
Once four brothers the power flowed equally.
Prod was counselor of Awarenn when Lillan
led is armies into Awarenn crushing them before their order.
The Orderion people were trained from birth
to lead a complete life of total order.
All of Awarenn accepted their fate.
They could not an would not fear.
For their awareness was the highest order.
Without fear death would never come.
The most respected code of Awarenn is this but a shield of honor?
Or may it be a peaceful nations silent war cry?
As they stood there looking onward and upward as they died.
Lillan's armies marched through taking Prod.
An both upon the platform Otar.
Prod spoke aloud, I am Prod counselor of Awarenn.
This you know, for we were once brothers.
We all gained great power an knowledge from Amen.
When he disbursed into our minds. An each of us
gained something in what we knew an to use
it in our own ways. Did Amen give this terror
to you Lillan of Orderion? Prod you fool.
I have found the book of Amen an in his own
words, laws were made to be broken so we can learn
justice without conception, don't you see he denied
his own faith. An destroyed himself an his own people.
Do you remember back when the four of us spoke of peace?
An I agreed as long as we were true. Amen an I were
close. He taught us all more than we can teach each other.

He told me once our world is just a soul an each part of the soul keeps the
other under their wing. We are balanced he said without one we will
never continue or without the other our existence will never have been.
For we are the dream. An I said Amen what's this concept? An he said
Lillan what's this order? For we are children in the mind of a child
searching for a god called Wisdom. It was then Atole spoke but one overstated
sentence an Amen turned his head. It was what Atole said. If we are
children of a mindless god, he is not a god yet he learns from us, he is a child
an we are his mind. An you said then we are searching for ourselves for we
are the wisdom makers an we are our own gods. An I asked Amen
if he knew this to be true an he laughed an said truth is a benign being
it shall destroy all things. I looked into his eyes his laugh was a cry
in disguise. He went off into the dark as I returned to my castle.
I looked back as it lit up the sky the Otar as all of Concepta
flashed an faded out of existence. An when I found his book his
last written words were. End the quest for wisdom for you have already
found it. Lillan I ask vigilance from you take care by your doings.
An know this Amen still exists but in our minds. We can make him
come to life by our thought. He's given us this power for a reason which you
know not. Each of us knows our fate. Each of us knows our end except you.
We shall always exist in our mind. Amen did not deny his faith he accepted
it as his end. We are all true to ourselves. An we are brothers together as
we are brothers alone. I accept my fate for I shall not die I shall live
forever. Prod we are all true but we are lying to ourselves. Forgive
me brother. Giveth me your awareness for I am to be aware. There I send
you to the wasteland you shall be consumed by Earth, Wind, Fire, an Water.
For now you are these things I say. I forgive you my brother. Vigilance
remember brother vigilance.

Chapter 2

Behold The Crystal Tower, Amen spoke of it in his words.
Amen tell me of your dream which you lived in the great tale.
Where all men were gods an all gods were men.
The tale of true life beyond. As The Tower radiated pure wisdom
into the hearts of all men that believed in an act
with the proven truth of all things entitled within the living
embodiment of a nature brought on by the high intellectual thought
process. Around The Tower they built glorious cities to invite
travelers of the cosmos. The lighting crystalized upon the
cities as from the stars you would see its creation as it looked
as the birth of life itself. A kingdom of light expanding forever
across a land known to be Low. Oh but Amen this is Low. As it is
Atole as it is. This is no future or no past nor present state of
time, it is here in our dreams. It exists as we do. For when
they sleep they dream of us. An when we sleep we dream of them.
This is but just a dream Amen. You'll learn Atole you'll learn. For
we are just the dream an as they are, being dreamed by others
in a distant dimension. We are their thoughts as they are ours, created
by thought of a higher conscious. We are of the mind. An in the
deep mind, which reaches into the vast void of spontaneous thought.
Atole we'll live forever in the mind through un-conceivable thought.
For this is the conception of retained thought.
We must stand beneath The Crystal Tower in our minds an feel
an learn its wisdom as I have an so must you. You believe you were
always here don't you Atole. We created you an all of Mentale.
So we together can complete the fourth plain of existence.
Remember we are one an you shall learn the tests as we learn them.

So I stand upon the Otar remembering our thoughts an what
we learned. As all of Concepta grows blacker than black. An
all of Awarenn stands in ruin an flames. As Lillan prepares
his soldiers to march upon mine own people of Mentale.
I wonder what shall be an there I thought I already know.
For Amen's thoughts are alive in mine as are Prods an Lillans.
I must go deeper into thought to learn of the fourth plain.
An see the tests as levels to pass teaching myself of the wisdom
shown to us in our dreams. In doing this I reveal it to them
as we are one. For this is a lesson to all creation, creating
the new.

There I call to you, I conjure from my own soul
an mine own thoughts to appear before me.
Speak unto me mighty Amen. Let our thoughts
become as one. Let us be as brothers again
an talk of the ancient talk. Let us learn of
the fourth plain together. For that which you
already know an I am to learn. For you wrote
the first laws which came to you through the dream.
Now show me the dream of dreams, the specter of specters,

the vision of visions, the shadow of shadows.
Let us see into the void reveal unto us your secrets
oh dominant force of Wisdom. Endow upon us your
potent knowledge. For you are the creator creating
the dream as are we creating the all-masterly thought.

Atole see the gate of wonder, cross through the door
of light. Step beyond all your bounds. Come with me
feel the radiance of wisdom. See what has been told
to you. Learn its true shape existing for the purpose
of enlightenment. You are seeing what you know.
You feel what you are. Look back it is you. See whom
is yourself. Contained within you are the truths
of Mentality, Awareness, Concept, an Order. An
all things bearing resemblance are the same.
You are the fourth plain of existence. Be you a god
as you are man.

Chapter 3

In that you know not the column.
It will come to you in time.
As you realize your apparent state
of being. In the realm of infinite
characterization. Lillan the
Deceitful One. Prod the Variant.
Amen a Cloud of Inversion.
An Atole the Instrument of
Completion.

There art thou who callith thy.
Through clouds of wonder.
An elucid sky of dreams.
Held by creation the ever continuing.
Pause - definitive ascendents.
Let us elaborate
in the pungence of procreation.
I am your answer
to undefined wisdom.

Look on as the bearing of bodies
in their present state of matter
all seem to be bound.
The object in question is translucent.
Its form of being is reluctantly silent.
An definitely it knows its existence.
The human eye sees what is as is.
We shall learn of its existence.
Therefore we must convert more time
an energy to this part of our mind
which we know not. As sometimes
you see something an it seems fine
but your mind is telling you
something is wrong with this picture.
In actuality this is the part of the mind
you must devote literally more attention to.
All have heard of the 6th sense.
Learn of it an learn of the mind.
What with more to help you understand the teachings.
The lessons of the plains.
The plains of existence.

Here we see the first plain of existence.
For man learned he could design.
Therefore attempting to create.
An what he created was the concept.
His concept was to evolve.
In this fashion blazing a trail.
Thus generalizing the next plains to come.

Take in mind the view of things that are to come.
Since they already are an already were.
Showing you these things are an will be.

Oh beith you a dream.
For I am the same.
You are a mystery an I am revelation.
Am I just a spectator
in this visible appearance of truth?
Master of the wiser.
Direct me into certain illuminance.
Lord of the legend.
The legend of Low.
An name me in affinity.
For I am an to be forever known to be Amen.
Harbinger of wisdom.

Here we see the second plain of existence.
For man learned he could control.
An what he controlled was the order.
His order was to organize.
Laying the foundations towards civilization.
A place of evident desire
which transcends the naturally limited state of all things.

Bare me a sword I will fight an conquer.
Bare me a shield an I will defend an harbour.
Bare me a helmet I will receive an become stronger.
For I am defiance standing in question.
Relying on fact I see no errors.
What do men seek but unity an control.
Lay aside your crown an watch.
See whom shall thrive to ware it.
Eliminate no one from exalted power.
None shall wear it except yourself.
Place the hand of perfection into the fire.
Does it burn not if it isn't flesh.
Why then shouldn't men look further?
An ask in himself of god.
Lord of the legend.
The legend of Low.
An name me in affinity.
For I am an forever known to be Lillan.
Statue of Prevalence.

Here we see the third plain of existence.
For man learned he could perceive.
An what he perceived was the consciousness.
His consciousness was to understand.
Thereby observing an helping others.
In this great quest to comprehend
unfounded an such highly phenomenal thought.

Giving reason to legible foundations.

All things can become separate from them selves.
Then all things can become as one again.
Forged together by unlimited forces of collective thought.
To try once more to pull together what seems the impossible.
These tests are hidden by confusion, anger, sadness, sorrow.
I feel the pains in you.
I hear the cries you release.
I see the terror raining fear.
I know the horror for I am aware.
Sovereigns of impalpable reactions.
Let this be known.
Only I can stand to be your cure.
Lord of the legend.
The legend of Low.
An name me in affinity.
For I am an forever known to be Prod.
Model of Redemption.

Here we see the fourth plain of existence.
For man learned he could recognize.
An what he recognized was the subconsciousness.
His subconscious was to evaluate.
For you become your own renderer of astonishment.
Revealing your own paths to perception.
Allowing yourself to enter the next plain
which has already been named.

Spiritualism is of the mind an soul.
It's within all of us.
But very few can acknowledge its existence.
Because they have never heightened their perception of things.
Through intellect an experience you'll break down the barriers
to countless doors through the mind.
We are warriors of thought.
Never to elude ourselves.
All spiritualists shall come to know themselves in time.
Where one learns another forgets.
Where one stands another falls.
Where one shouts another cries.
Where one lives another dies.
Lord of the legend.
The legend of Low.
An name me in affinity.
For I am an forever known to be Atole.
Keeper of The Legacy.

Through the skull, through the mind, through the eyes - exploding, exploding.
Crossing time backwards we travel.
Lost inside where we appear.
The first score reveled The Earth.
Behind dark walls of concealment.
The light cast a shadow.
Rumble oh tolerant one.
Cracking dawn shuffled the temblor.

Dry an baron lands of nothing.
Where am I in such a place,
such a world? I laugh as I search.
Is it here shall I find what I seek?
Do I know what I am to find?
A wilderness of the first part.

Here are the remnants of our past of our future.
Where no life exists not even I for I am only the seer.
I take in my hand the dirt from this ground.
It is of me, it is of you but it is cold no warmth
no comfort shall be found here only sands.
Sands of the covering stratum.

The link I have made here
will stir the silent calls of the shadow
which shall never disappear.
So then we'll never leave here.
-
No presence of life.
Non-existency found by me.
Rattle of silence.
Soundless visions.

I know things.
Things that would
change your heart
change your mind.

Things that would
change your pulse
change your life.

Commit me to this world.
For I am the same.
Here I found in it the void.
Where unspeakable truths
shout their cries in latent silence.
Plunder an pulverize
through the beckons of time.

It's only to pass.
It's only to come.

Distant roads to no where
lie in the amidst's of the mountain's lair.
I've only one path to follow.
That is of my own.
Who shall track, my footsteps?
In the heat of the day?
In the cold of the night?
Who shall follow, in my footsteps?
Where I've gone, you shall come.
Where I've been, you shall be.
Where I've begone, you shall know.
Track the setting sun.
Track the rising moon.
Track the stars
mapping the land.
Crossing, crossing, crossing.

Your journey is only yet to begin.
Only you know the trails to come.
What you seek you shall find.
What shall you find, your destiny.

Some may come to know the land as their own.
Some may look further into desolate utopias.
An you may be lost without the civilization you know.
So you find your way back to what you call home.
Then there will be those who never look back.
Chasing the sun even in their dreams.
For what they have found, besieged by the limitless an free.
Their children will, hath come to know life
upon the mouth of creation, where in they'll look onward.
Where in what has come shall pass then come again.
Then they as they've grown will follow in the footsteps of the setting sun.
Some may be-seat in the palaces of the mountains lair.
Some may bend to the wilting grotto at hand.
Making new what has turned an become as sand.
With them they'll bring only the legends
they themselves help make during the last turn of the sands.

What is this that's crossing?
An indigenous pre-historic creature.
Following its own journey of life.
Look, look what do we see here?
That's been uncovered, smashed, an revealed by fate.
Through the eyes, through the mind, through the skull.

Chapter 5

All seems to be lost, my mind is clouded I can't seem to think.
The Otar half destroyed my city in flames, men screaming
men dying I feel their pain. War is loose who opened
the cage. Not only but I. Who am I to make decisions
in such a manner. Our women fighting, our children
fighting everyone dying. Lillan we now face oblivion.
What shall become of us only what's become of them.

War makes peace an peace makes war.
Warring are the fighters gone to war.
Named the pirates of the light.

Flames, blood, swords Oh does the earth shake.
Oh does our temples crumble upon us.
The sky lit just as day.
Night shouts screaming bloody war.
Tell it to go away.
Lillan your order is great.
My mentality can't be saved.
Atole, Atole help us Atole.

God of Wisdom.
Where is my path?
Where is my truth?
Is my name not Atole?
If you are the merciful-all?
If you are the indestructible?
Help us break the dream.
This nightmare that plagues us.
Am I not the same?
I am Atole master of the game.

Enter, enter. All enter.
The convocation of the mind.
I charge, the power in the Otar.
Return us to the brink of primordial times.
Quiet the sounds of thunder.
Pivot children into my arms.
Feel my warmth an love.
For I give you strength an you give me the same.
Come my people give strength in love.
Let us sing Valhalla for those that were slain.
An let us leave this world, this reality, this plain.

Atole you'll never escape.
Until you prove truth in our names.
Prove that we are the same.
Brother, this will not be in vein.

Don't it feel like tomorrow's day will never have been.
Only when sorrow's lost may you begin.
Sometimes there's no more.
Sometimes it seems all is done.
When you awake an know this day will be the same.
I can't live life knowing this pain.

Don't it feel like you've lost in a game
that you didn't want to play.
When men live an men die.
Only when sadness plays.
A dream can not be saved.
Revel behind all that stands in your way.
Envy must take its part.
Reliving making no mistakes.

Standing in the isle.
Looking at them stand in line.
Realizing you're in the same line.
I hate to be me.
Seeing whom is he.
Fighting the flee.
Here I leave behind my legacy.

This paper soaks the ink in clear.
As the words mean all inside.
You learn from my thought.
I learn from my thought.
Wiping away the fabric of reality.
For it's what's beneath that stands to listen.
I abide a law buried in time.
In these thoughts you know the strain.
Man laughs at his dream.
An god laughs with his dream.
I represent a status of preparation.
In the flight of your spiritual evolution.

Stray no longer, thee are lost alone.
Stand within, hunter of choice.
Be calm yet vile in strike.
Seek the thought barring no question.
I hold you in heart man as women.
I hold you in spite whence your deeds have done.
Love with prayer be it a sacrifice.
Licking the body as it bites.
Blood is pure you who are all brothers.
No death shall be a slaying.
Yet it's done by all your own right.
I am of no state selecting whom I love.
I am of no state selecting whom I hate.
For it is of the forces speaking the question.
I know not the separation of whom is male or female.
Yet it exists you are the same in my eyes.
Love whom you love for it is only what an how it makes you feel inside.
Therefore prayer is question holding no love.

You shall be judged within your own mind.
For what you believe shall condone your spirit.
An you shall live an die knowing your own pain.
Only to learn the key to the next plain.
An where upon you return you shall be changed.

All those who stand with me
will come to know the satire
whence all men acquire.

This pen draws the ink in clear.
For it is different each time.
As a child begins his quest for knowledge
who do they consult their parents.
An when an adult ends his quest for knowledge
who do they consult their gods.

Therefore you never end your quest.
It's only just beginning.

There is only one fallacy in creation.
It is the hidden things all men seek.
For those things cause all suffering.
Advancing mankinds abilities to learn.
Thereby tapping every source to obtain knowledge.
An where he can't explain he'll fill in the blanks.
This is known as the question.
Many will answer this question as truth.
You may even substitute one as the other.

I've no doubt in my unearthly mind
that man's life is becoming distant from within itself.
The deeper I delve into my thoughts, bare judgement.
I understand the communion.
For it is something stating the non-acceptance.
When all is together it shall be a part of itself.

Too many have come.
They've heard but do not see.
Too many have gone.
They've seen but they do not hear.
What shall become of them?
Those who are silent.
Those who are chosen to stand within.
Be this the call to recollection.
All those who are the same shall endeavor my thought.

Covet what is in my hand.
For it is yours.
What I reveal to you
may be utter devastation.
Then to another is truly a solemn gift.
Tranquility lies within.

Make pure an establish from mine own covenant.
The hand of sacrifice is extended.
Know thy from what you can interpret.
The laws of continuance
support the foundations for all structures.
What you learn becomes the laws.
Then you can raise the walls.
There by closing in your great tome.
En-sealed an mounted upon the sands of time.

Chapter 7

Come Lillan, come walk with me into the serenity.
An let us carry-out our prestige together.
Let us arrive binding our laws once more.
Let us make peace where there is war.
For this has all been done before.
As you're right I shall never escape.
No escape mechanism shall hide us.
It's only that the truths been seen.
By you an by me now it's time.
Let's let all things be.

Everything has a place.
I'm prepared to put everything in its place.
Are you Lillan of Orderion?

Atole this is foolish.
Just surrender.
Then all will be replaced.
Can't you hear the silent laughs?
It's them who are gone from us.
Amen an Prod they laugh.
I must finish the game.

An then so Lillan.
The game will finish itself.
I'm haunting you Lillan.
I'm haunting you.
Your mind will never be at rest.
-
Oh Southern Star.
Where am I to go?
Where am I to fly?
Oh my body.
Disassemble me.
Lay me in a coffin.
Lower me into my grave.
Cosmic descention awaits.

It's the funeral of the gods.
Eternal rest shall come.
Arising through the mystic reveal.
A haunting of the body.
Laid to rest in shallow tomes.
I've the eyes to guide you through.

You see all these.
Those who will never sleep.
A tainted river.
For those who can not see.

I've the mine, the knowing that's true.
Lillan hear my thoughts.
For we are the same.
See with me the truths of all things.
See not with your eyes.
But see with your mind.
Your mind's eye.

Let us enter
following the dream.
Travel, travel with me.
Through endless eternity.
See what's been done before.
An it shall be done again.

Atole what world is this?
Where we find countless paradise
upon the shores of the setting sun.
An lives know no end.

Here is where only we can go.
Thriving together as one.
The whole is a part.
An the part is a whole.
For we've never left.
It's all here part of the great dream.
As real as any you've ever seen.

Now Lillan tell me what you see.
Parallel worlds of looping winds.
Where is that paradise now?
What I create I can destroy.
What you create you can destroy.
Then we together can create it all over again.
A thousand lessons to be learned.
In a hundred turns.
-
They know time.
I know time.
Now you know time.
They know death.
I know death.
Now you know death.
Space an time.
It's all in all.
Time melts away.
Space divides itself.
Maximum parallel exceeds separation.
Direct onto the angle.
Where one sits the other intrudes.
Twenty could be ten.
An ten could be forty.

Once said always was.
If heard to be known.

Buried there are man's remains.
Buried here is the secrets.
Foretelling man's mortal remains.
The law of life is life.
The law of death is death.
I saw the score in times said.
I saw the score in times done.
I saw the score in times to come.
For time folds in on itself.
It could be a thousand years from tomorrow.
It could be a thousand years from yesterday.
It could be a thousand years within today.
The tower of continuance stands high.
It contains the spiritual an intellectual levels
in which you shall attain in the hereafter an the here to come.
These plains lie in our minds.
But it's only here we unlock the doors.
Leading us into the emittion of the divine center.
The whole of everything is within.
You shall learn the paths.
You shall learn the roads.
You may even learn the shortcuts.
Breaking down the barriers.
Reaching your highest point within the column.

Work your magic pen held tightly in my hand.
Work it from my body, from my soul, from my mind.
People tend to overlook the things you'll never see.
An even if you did you could not interpret what it means.
It's just what you have to look for at the right time.
When you find it discover its truth an name it for what it is.

If it be treachery name it as so.
An never forget what it means.
Eliminate it with subtle glory.

If it be illusion name it as so.
An never forget what it means.
Eliminate it with absolute reassurance.

If it be corruption name it as so.
An never forget what it means.
Levy it with distinct disruption.

If it be heresy name it as so.
An never forget what it means.
Correlate it with manic resolution.

Some things may all be forgotten an some never shall.

What you use in every day nature determines this.
Take to mind the use of such thought.
Leaves man at vibrant ends eluding sanity.
You become as feeble as when you began.
Must you know that only tolerance brings you control.
An when you establish contact make it known.
Unless you've a plan to overcome.
By wit, by genuine thought trained for the unknown.

Here is love it has its name.
Never forget it's of its own.
Accept it or abolish it.
By opening to it or letting it go.

Here is hate it has its name.
Never forget it's of its own.
Counter it or allow it.
By learning what made it so or forgetting what you know.
To some this will be a heavy burden in its longing to find out why.
To others they'll be careless an laugh at the whims of those who spout hatred.

Here is ridicule its name is that.
Never forget it is its own.
Belittle it with mora justice.
An rapture with might in arms.

Here is embarrassment its name is that.
Never forget it becomes its own.
Render it with appeasement expelling regret.
For if you know these things never lagging you've entered a plain who's name is that.

There are a multitude of questions.
There are a multitude of answers.
If I were to reveal them all at this point
I would leave you no where to go.
An leave myself in shallow echos.
For your path is long.
An even longer if you were to look back.
Each thing we'll learn together.
Each thing we'll learn alone.
For your quest will take you further
then anything you've come to know.
It shall all be recorded.
An passed on to the sons an daughters.
Who shall call upon the forbidden moment
which lies within, their growing souls.
Carrying with them golden dreams to be fulfilled.

I have the confidence in myself.
To push me further an further ahead.
Striving on because I believe in me.
An I will accomplish my goals.

If I have found myself in me
then I have found me in myself.
For I am free to be whom I shall be.

Through the skull, through the mind, through the eyes.
Exploding, exploding.
Crossing time backwards we travel.
Lost inside where we appear.
The second score reveled the wind.
Behind dark walls of concealment.
The light cast a shadow.
Whirl oh tolerant one.
Spinning vortex funneled the air.

Dry an baron lands of nothing.
Where am I in such a place.
Such a world, I laugh as I search.
Is it here shall I find what I seek?
Do I know what I am to find?
A wilderness of the second part.

Here are the remnants of our past of our future.
Where no life exists not even I for I am only the seer.
I take in my lungs the air from this space.
It is of me, it is of you but it is cold no warmth
no comfort shall be found here only winds.
Winds of the covering stratum.

The link I have made here
will stir the silent calls of the shadow
which shall never disappear.
So then we'll never leave here.
-
No presence of life.
Non-existency found by me.
Rattle of silence.
Soundless visions.

I know things.
Things that would
change your heart
change your mind.

Things that would
change your pulse
change your life.

Commit me to this world.
For I am the same.
Here I found in it the void.
Where unspeakable truths
shout their cries in latent silence.
Plunder an pulverize

through the beckons of time.
It's only to pass.
It's only to come.

Dreamland exists, only if you can find it.
They've come from afar, from distant worlds.
To land their selves in time, in our time.
Once we've come to know them, never forget.
They track on under scorching heat.
An smelding winds of furry.
Following the crackled ground.
Tracing the footsteps of man.
An what they've come to find.
Leaves all in desperate hands.

I walk on an on an on.
Another mile, farther away.
I've traveled a long long way.
Blazed my trails in these boots.
Carving a path into the sun.
Now I am tired of moving my feet.
Taking step after step.
Following the wind.
One more step an I will die.
It's only one more step away.

I can not believe
once I was a man.
Wandering the earth
in the footsteps of life.
Leaving behind the mark of the boot.

The Human Skull

Was a man was a man.
The skull is all they'll find.
He left them all a thousand years behind.

Was a man was a man.
Ever so was a man.
A man of flesh.
The flesh of life.
A life so grim.

So there ist thou the gift of life.
Forgotten in time we move backward
upon an ancient burial ground.
As time has shown man to be a spectacle of life.
In his tome his weary grave.
He has fallen beyond.
Entering earth so boldly discovering.
Does he know death?
A place for men of flesh.

Was a man was a man.
Gone forever was he there?
Removing the dirt from below.
Raising it up high.
Looking into the eyes of the skull.

Chapter 10

Amen here is your great book of laws.
Where are you now to employ them?
I deem this book question.
For I am Lillan of Orderion.
I now exercise dominion over all of Low.
All that is to the east.
All that is to the west.
An to the north an to the south.

All shall know my furry.
For I take none as my own.
You will hear the screams
thought only that would come through nightmares.
Your children will know the end before the beginning.
An you will surely know death as all life ends.
For I bring war because peace has been broken.
None shall escape for I am determined by fate.

Listen here, listen to the words of your wisdom maker.
Are world is dead never born, never begun.
Time is spent in shrewd games.
This here is the dream of names.
Names of borrowing content, some where a dream will break.
A higher conscious will wake, we will only be memories fading out of date.
This here I've proven, never revealed because this is our fate.

But Lillan we shall always be here.
Through the pages of history.
Through the annals of time.
We will only be forgotten
if we let them forget us.
Amen knew you would find his book.
It was the only way to teach us.
His final lesson an that he's done.

An that I have done Atole.
For time catches up with itself.
Amen, may this be you?
See Atole you speak to apparitions.
For you are out of body, out of mind.
Lillan it was Amen, he spoke unto me.
Prove this truth you've declared.
I can only show you what you know.
If you do not believe then maybe you never will.
I must prove nothing to you or no one else.
What I must prove is my truth in myself.
An I've learned my own. Now it's time that you do the same.
When you learn of an within, you'll stand back
an become as a whole again.

The Nightmare

I've awaken once more.
Yet I ask why, I am to die?
Life is burning me.
So I can't go back there.
I know the horror.
For I can still see their faces.

You'll awaken to realize, that death is there
waiting for you, it's coming.
Can't you hear the flutes?

Stand back an listen, I am The Nightmare.
Your nightmare, coming true.

I've been so calm, I'm patiently waiting.
Now it's time, I'll take you.

Cremation of the flesh.
Human remains burnt to dust.
Blow upon the ashes.
Cloudy mass, swirling
out of incarnation.
-
I've seen the chariots
riding in the wind.
Traveling on.
Riding so far.
Carrying away
the dead's soul, so far
into the nothing.
Racing with time.
Blazing a trail
through this warrior's mind.

Carry me away.
Chariots of the sun.
Fly so high.
Take me to the sky.

Back from the unknown.
It seems I have past away.
Some where I wandered.
But who's to say.
I am a ghost.
I am a spirit.
I am a demon
back from the grave.
Tomorrow's waiting there.
A place of dredge an ware.

Strengis Believis in the god of deathis.

I am Strengis.
Believer in the god of death.
I know the tales
from whence only horror prevails.

I am a soldier.
Believer in the blood of men.
I know the wars
from whence I have come.

For I have come from battle.
A place of death.
Where no one survive.
Scattered dead, across the fields.
Lying are the men, born to die.

What scripture is this that speaks words in crippling twilight?
An to many flowering happiness as words are poems in themselves.
I cast a shadow in the eyes of man as woman.
This shadow is truth an let truth be known.
I am to love, I am to make peace, an I am to be happy.
In my own ways I shall make them of me.
You my people of your own will do the same.
Convicting your soul to these needs.
An where an when this is lost then again.
I cast a shadow in the eyes of man as woman.
This shadow is truth an let truth be known.
I am to hate, I am to make war, an I am to be sad.
In my own ways I shall make them of me.
You my people of your own will do the same.
Convicting your soul to these needs.

Flow ink of this pen like a river
never ending till then.
When all is lost, when no more are born.
This dimension as we know it will close.
What will be left is what is here.
An when again it's found a mystery will be revealed.

Can lives last longer then found.
Can dreams last longer then made.
Can visions last longer then seen.
Can spirits last longer than known.

Arbitrarily fact stands as question.
I put this to rest with a question.
Why then upon the arenas of conflict
does each sides evidence leave no
interpreting evidence except what
was known at first start. Tracing
the footsteps backwards until you
hit a wall where the forces truly
state a question within itself.
Then fear is what results of the unknown.
An then satire animates recklessness.
Thereby allowing holy wars to become as truth.

Wasting no time religious intervention clouds all truths.
Laying way to the wastelands of this reality.
I come as man, I come as truth.
Seen through the eyes of discontent.
Your god exists but within you.
For I am god an so are you.
The higher you raise your spiritual level
is the closer you will be to yourself.

No mortal being can rest
until spiritually you are one again.
Then you shall descend cosmically.
Then a second flight will be engaged.
Your dreams will have been long, eternity.
Some may have gone together.
Some may have gone alone.
But you'll return as it shows
in what you have learned.
Here is a riddle which shall shake an crumble
all unstable foundations, supported by question.
What ties the ties ending
that which tied the ties beginning.

Through the skull, through the mind, through the eyes.
Exploding, exploding.
Crossing time backwards we travel.
Lost inside where we appear.
The third score reveled the fire.
Behind dark walls of concealment.
The light cast a shadow.
Flare oh tolerant one.
Plight an smitten with burning ignition.

Dry an baron lands of nothing.
Where am I in such a place,
such a world, I laugh as I search.
Is it here shall I find what I seek?
Do I know what I am to find?
A wilderness of the third part.

Here are the remnants of our past of our future.
Where no life exists not even I for I am only the seer.
I take in my eyes the flames these visions of heat.
It is of me, it is of you but it is cold no warmth
no comfort shall be found, here are only fires.
Fires of the covering stratum.

The link I have made here
will stir the silent calls of the shadow.
Which shall never disappear.
So then we'll never leave here.

No presence of life.
Non-existency found by me.
Rattle of silence.
Soundless visions.

I know things.
Things that would
change your heart
change your mind.

Things that would
change your pulse
change your life.

Commit me to this world.
For I am the same.
Here I found in it the void.
Where unspeakable truths
shout their cries in latent silence.
Plunder an pulverize

through the beckons of time.
It's only to pass.
It's only to come.
Bringith me your troubles.
An I will show them to you.
Takeith away the pain
that crosses the dyeing mill.
Let me father your predestined lives.
I shall replenish the fire in your vein.
An make abundant the armours of luxury.
As we lie in wait for the great freeze.
Time shall honor you with descention or inclination.
Then erasure of the mind will permit no remembrance.
Though you still attain your level to be heightened further.
Through return by inclination of willing factor.
At the last moments of breath you'll think god, your god.
It will be the union of yourself within, the divine center.

Out of body.
I am the wizard of time.
I am the wind maker.
An fire burning into your mind.

Smell the fresh earth
dug from the ground.
Taste the air.
Listen for the unsound.
I'm dead, waiting
for the rebirth.

Out of body.
Out of time.
Out of life.
Out of mind.

Herrivy Cole

I stand with you
when you're alone.
You close your eyes
an what do you see?
Nothing, that is me.
I am the Herrivy Cole
something trapped
deep within your dreams.

Did I choose to be here?
Did I even have a choice?
Man is his own enemy
fighting himself.
Fighting his own thoughts.
Drawn up by the mind.
Why do you think
you think twice?
For the nothing will be.
Then we shall meet.

Salvage is hopeless.
Something that can not be fought.
Nothing, can ease the pain.
Where did it come from?
Where did it subscribe my name?

How can you know?
I am the Herrivy Cole
of this life, ever so.

Can you decipher, what this means?
As I place these pieces of bone fragment together.
Can you see the end come?
Can you see the emptiness enter when it comes?
Then you bring it with you when you come.
This I'll tell you there are times of escape
yet there is no escape. An there are times
of remembrance yet there is no remembrance.
You must then look deeper an gather it from within.
Look people an look children look here.
Look through the eyes, through the mind, through the skull.

Through the skull, through the mind, through the eyes.
Exploding, exploding.
Crossing time backwards we travel.
Lost inside where we appear.
The fourth score reveled the water.
Behind dark walls of concealment
the light cast a shadow.
Embark oh tolerant one.
New life cascaded from the fountains fall.

Dry an baron lands of nothing.
Where am I in such a place,
such a world I laugh as I search.
Is it here shall I find what I seek?
Do I know what I am to find?
A wilderness of the fourth part.

Here are the remnants of our past of our future.
Where no life exists not even I for I am only the seer.
I take in my body the storm from this milky pool.
It is of me, it is of you but it is cold no warmth
no comfort shall be found here only waters.
Waters of the covering stratum.

The link I have made here
will stir the silent calls of the shadow.
Which shall never disappear.
So then we'll never leave here.

No presence of life.
Non-existency found by me.
Rattle of silence.
Soundless visions.

I know things.
Things that would
change your heart
change your mind.

Things that would
change your pulse
change your life.

Commit me to this world.
For I am the same.
Here I found in it the void.
Where unspeakable truths
shout their cries in latent silence.

Plunder an pulverize
through the beckons of time.
It's only to pass.
It's only to come.
An what does water do?
It flows, it moves, it embarks.
From some where it's come
to nurture life.
For you may have to find the end
before you find the beginning.

It was there I traveled, before I shut my eyes.
I looked as I lay dying in the sands. Was it
there? A current of flowing water as clear as
the sky that I once knew. It has become as night
around me. I must drag my withered an restless
body made of mortal flesh on, to this place of renascence.
To refresh my crying soul. Let it not be a mirage or I
shall crack under the sun. Dripping blood of thirst
an hunger. Forever longing for comfort in the setting sun.

May this be what I've found. Let me drink an wet
my face. What has happened the current has taken
me. I'm falling, I'm falling. What are these
dreams I see? Are they of my life of my past lives?
Where is it taken me? Though I feel free as if I'm
flying as if I'm shooting through the distant sun.

Where am I, I can now see the stars as I'm
moving tor'ds a light. An I can see three other
currents moving into it. I'm almost there.
I'm closing in. Look at this, what I can see.
Through the eyes, through the mind, through the skull.

Chapter 14

So Lillan we return from the dream. I have learned
many things an you what have you learned? I have seen
into this vision an pulled from it my own truth. That
what I am is lost without our whole. [But Lillan
look again we are a whole; are unit is complete.
Yes Lillan we are. Prod, you're of flesh not a spirit
in my nightmare come to life? That I am for you are
my own vindicator as you were my executioner. Look
in your hands what do you hold but the earth
of this land, an of me. Now let it be of me. Atole
look there what is that, that makes the clouds
move? Which you breathe from an to. Let your
breath be of mine. [An I give you the fire in
my eyes. Amen, be this a dream? The dream
of dreams, Lillan. Now I absorb from the
clouds the water to soothe the fire as we've
all learned truth. I ask forgiveness from
you three for I've learned dignity. Don't ask
for forgiveness Lillan. We are all still Brothers together
as we are Brothers alone. You've made your peace
now be free. Come now, come walk with me an let us
complete the dream by ending it with a new
beginning. We are in unison let us hold hands
an recite are names an who an what we are.

Let us raise the tower, The Crystal Tower.
For I am Amen, Harbinger of Wisdom.
For I am Lillan, Statue of Prevalence.
For I am Prod, Model of Redemption.
For I am Atole, Keeper of The Legacy.

Let's gather the sheep.
Bring, in the, herds of the night.
Scatter their dreams.
In pale shades of light.
Enter the sonic sleep.

Past voyage, proceeding time.
Catch onto, the wave.
Don't let time, pass you by.
Seen from, the other-side.
We are ascending, yet falling.
Coming down, as, new day showers.
All hail, the rising, of, The Crystal Tower.

An when it arose their eyes widened.
Awakening them to the truths of the world.
An they stood back an looked on.
Thinking of the black shroud which was cast upon them.
Buy who's chance did this come about?
Yet by their own blindness they deceived themselves.
This marked their end.
Then it was him who saw through all.
I cast away the blind shadow.
All those who know the way through
will come unto thy an seek the column.

-

Melting away the terror.
It marked their end.
Melting away the pain.
It marked their beginning.
An remember who said
I will end this madness.
Being the truth lies in your mind.
See the tower rising from the flames.

What is this?
A place of life.
A place of death.
What keeps us here?
In this hell.
What is that?
Telling us to live.
Just one more day.
Why should we suffer as man as woman?
In a life we don't want.
Why should we suffer?
In a world that's not.

When you know your dream is dead
you just keep on going day by day.
Wonder, on in pain, why does it
have to be this way?
Wonder, on in pain, why does life
twist us insane?

Was it me, am I the accused?
Did I murder someone?
Did I leave them mangled in pieces?
Please tell me, was it me?
Why keep me in this prison?
Am I trapped here for eternity?
Somehow, somewhere.

I will find you, the one
who put me here.

It was from then on, I searched.
I learned an faced my fears.
In every step closer, I felt to be thrown off the path.
My will is stronger than I've come to believe.
It was the forces pulling an pulling
from side to side as they were two of one.
Then suddenly some how, some way
I merged them in my mind, eternity.
My fogged visions became clear, so clear.
Laid out in front of me, like I was guided.
Pushed day in an day out to capture their essence
in these pages, for this is my destiny.
What I found there which is here was myself.
All shall come to know yourself.
It is then your destiny will become clear.
-

Destiny

Your dream is your destiny.
What you see is your dream.
It stands to be far from you.
Yet it is closer then you know.
Some may give up an let it go.
An some may try again.
If you're going to fulfill your destiny
don't try to do it, just make it happen.
It's all within you, remember that.
When all is lost hope is around the corner.
Face your fear an fly away free from your chains.
Your mind knows success therefore you shall succeed.
-
Each step I took, each thing that happened
an each thing I went through, it all seemed
to be a test. As if I was testing myself.
For sometimes I'd say I'm not ready for this,
I don't want to do this, I can't do this.
In actuality I could an I did. I proved
to myself I was capable of handling an
dealing with things. Not to forget I
was being pushed from behind the entire way.
As I said guided through. That's what everyone
needs a little push from behind. To get them
motivated. In this redundantly baffled
game of life. Now can you find all
the pieces. Perfection comes with divine
talent.

Perfection

There are many things wrong in this world.
If you can separate what you know.
You know what is right.
Though to others it can be wrong.
Therefore only judge yourself.
For what you believe can only be true.
That what you feel is only what I feel
except in a different perspective.
What one does in their life
makes them feel right.
Unless you are caught in-between.
You can't choose what is right or wrong.
Never can you place any blame.
For no one is perfect
except perfection within itself.

Spiritual Dimensional Plains
all around us part of the fabric
ending the seems torn open.
By a single spark known as life
tearing the window wide open
just as death opens it.
Once open allowing creation
to admit the force; then so
dearly an ever so that force
fights to survive. With all
the energy built up only a
percentage is used. The rest
comes back against you. The
same force protecting an helping
you is the same which will
break you down an finally
destroy you. Just as you
see a spark of fire it's alive
in its own form. The same
force igniting it. Opening
the window for a split second.
Devours its own energy with
its other as the same. Seals
the window closing the gate
to the other. So much force is
put into igniting
an keeping it ignited it
burns itself out. This is
inevitable. Just as it's inevitable
as all men live they shall die.
Unless a new plain is created
or discovered.

The vivid marker that bares life
shows me I'm something direct.
I told you to trace the edge
along the thin line of sanity.
No one calls on me.
For I went into the angle
made by the four points of light.
It's name was dealt by me.
The column strictly defines it.
For I am the horizontal.
An I am the vertical.
I am the sphere.
As I am the shadow.

For this is the formula
engraved on the second shield.
My seal, the seal of time.
There in lies two hour glasses, which coincide.
You'll find the past, present, future.
An the void or space, even spirit world.
That which holds the four angles.
An remember the pyramid.
For it represents time.
An some in your visions
might see a crystal of this form.
Forever turning, an forever glowing.

See through the vision, the double shield.
See that which is an what was.
For I am he who's coming
marks the day when all truths shall be known.
An all falsehoods shall be exposed.

The Mastered

When a man lives deep within himself
watching the world from behind his cold eyes.
Seeping terror out of his very stare
knowing man's corruption leaving him baron.
They don't see him for what he stands.
For they live in a world outside themselves.
Never knowing the true meaning of life.
An all they know is what the call reality.
But is it there around them a world created from the mind?
A life without apparent cause they are afraid of him.
Afraid he will show them what they already know.
Denying every thought that will dissolve their dream.
So he watches an waits laughing at their world.
Delusional people wandering in circles.
Controlled by the creators creating the dream.
From whence time is entaled I see something.
An that I name a tree now analogued in my brain for all eternity.
Intelligence named for knowing be it there a man without a dream.
Gone forth in time seen the misery laid in a path.
Let there be creation where the creators don't exist.
Call him insane if you wish an hope he finds a cure for your plague.
Onward in death he will go so called the end of life.
There is no heaven there is no hell.
An there is no god keeping all well.
Look among you a man you will fear with the knowing.
For he is the new creator the only god rising from your reality.
He who has solved the almighty mystery.
He who has broken the dream reality.

The Dream

We walked the street in the dream.
I saw them each at a different place.
As I seen them cry as I moved on, was I dead?
One's name I heard was it (++++).
An one's name was it (++++).
There's the third I can't remember.
I know the faces but why do they cry?
Is it because I left behind?
They wanted me to stay with them.
An so did I, for some reason I still moved on.
An I wanted to cry, so I did.
My tears brought rain an the night sky.
I wandered an thought over, why?
Is it because I'm alive?
Then a man appeared an said
I have the solution.
An that's all he said.
For I seen as one girl stood by my side
an one by my other.
There it was her waving goodbye.
An I dropped my head, she was the third.
I know, I've seen her cry, a love that can not die.
Was this the last I'd ever see her?
We walked the street in the dream.

We entered the great safe.
Downward the guide shown us through.
They offered us material items in giant paper titles.
An I said, what is this place?
Then he said, the warehouse.
The store selling life.
An I said, what will it cost?
An he said, for free.
I realized it was my own life
being sold before me.
What I took I don't remember.
It's what I'll gain while I'm living.

There we were driving in the night.
What we saw was a great light.
As it became clear a giant cloud appeared.
The light came so fast as I looked.
I said, this is the end.
Lowering my head an closing my eyes.
It hit as I felt it, I entered the nothing.
My existence had ended, I saw nothing.
I felt nothing, I heard nothing.
I was trapped, then I awoke.
I had returned, saying aloud
like a nuclear bomb.

From there the dream had twisted in.
Their flesh was rotten, I could see no faces.
We were seven there as men.
An those decaying bodies were many.
Escape was impossible, forced into the caged room.
Darkness was our cover as we lit the torches.
We knew they would come.
Some how one of us must survive
to tell the story, to come back alive.
As they pounded on the dry rotted doors
an smashed them, some tried to come
in through the caged windows.
As some windows were blocked other were clear.
-

Then one spoke up.
One of us must survive.
I will bare a sword
an protect the boy child.
If I die there will
be six here as men.
-

Then another spoke.
One of us must survive.
I will swing the torch
an blaze a trail.
If I die there will
be five here as men.

Yet another spoke.
One of us must survive.
I will hurl these chains
an spread them out.
If I die there will
be four here as men.
-

Still another.
One of us must survive.
I will smash them with these rocks
an blind them so they can't fight.
If I die there will
be three here as men.
-

An then on.
One of us must survive.
I will attack them with my fists
until I can't raise my arms.
If I shall die there will
be two here as men.
-

Then the boy stood tall.
Looking towards me.
One of us must survive.

I will yell loud with my voice
an deafen them as I scream the song of our flight.
If I die there will
be one of us here as men.
Then I spoke inside as I cried.
One of us must survive.
I will sacrifice my life
distracting the castellan.
If I shall die there will
be none here as men.
-
They went separate ways
breaking out of there.
The creature was mighty.
Going after the boy an swordsman.
At the gate as I came out
he came after me as I called
him. Castellan, laughing
at me I struggled to sway
from his sharp plunges.
Finally, his scepter pierced my flesh an I fell.
I seen them run through the gate.
Two completed the flight.

Daddy, what's in the dark?
Everything that's in the light, my child.
Everything that's in the light.